TOP SECRET

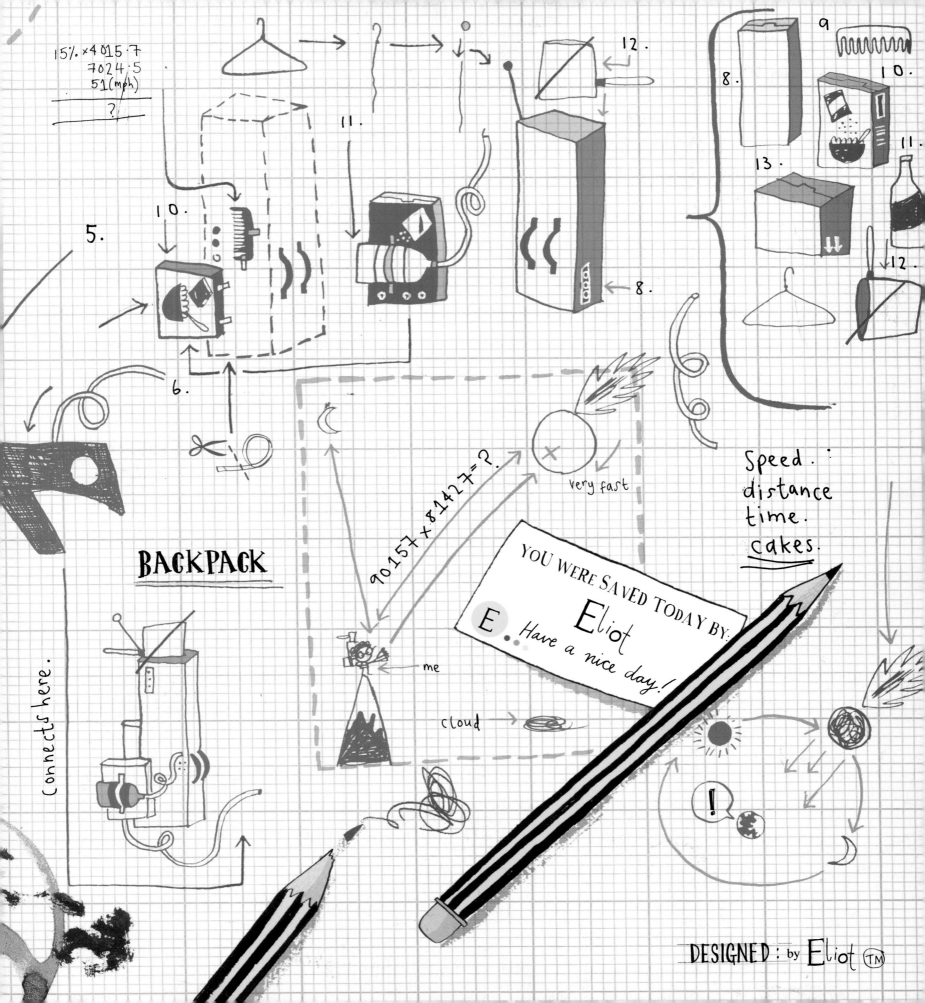

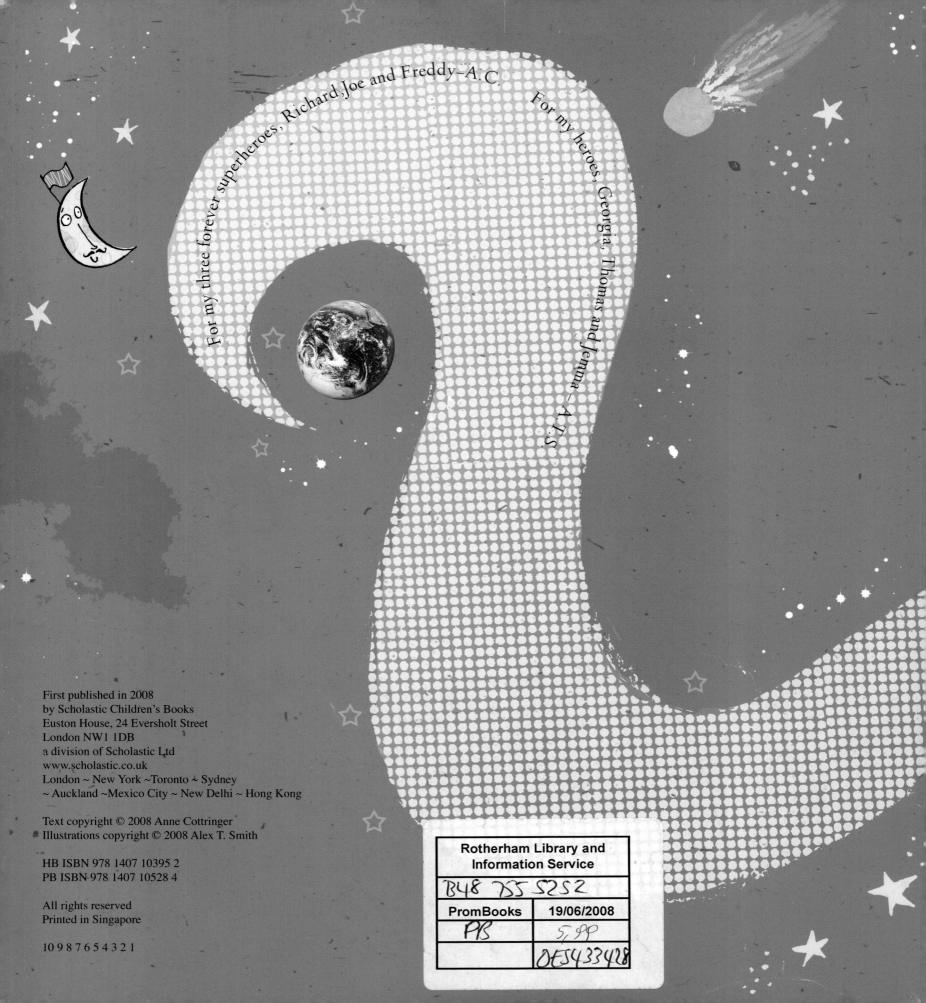

For my three forever superheroes, Richard, Joe and Freddy~A.C.

For my heroes, Georgia, Thomas and Jemma~A.T.S

First published in 2008
by Scholastic Children's Books
Euston House, 24 Eversholt Street
London NW1 1DB
a division of Scholastic Ltd
www.scholastic.co.uk
London ~ New York ~Toronto ~ Sydney
~ Auckland ~Mexico City ~ New Delhi ~ Hong Kong

HB ISBN 978 1407 10395 2
PB ISBN 978 1407 10528 4

10 9 8 7 6 5 4 3 2 1

ELIOT JONES, MIDNIGHT SUPERHERO

By day,
Eliot is quiet.
He reads his books.
He feeds his goldfish.
He watches Mr Smith
wash his car.

TIBET

TOY BOX

"Eliot
is such a
quiet little
thing,"
say all the
grownups.

Tick! Tock! Tick! Tock!
Tick! Tock!

BONG!

But when the clock
strikes *midnight*...

Eliot is a superhero!

He hangs out of
helicopters.

He skis down glaciers.

He returns teddies
to babies.

Eliot

Sometimes the mayor needs Eliot's help.

"The lions have escaped from the zoo!" he cries. "They're rampaging through the streets!"

Luckily, Eliot is an expert lion tamer.

He leaps from his bedroom window, races through the screaming crowds...

...and comes face to face with the lions.
He stares into the eyes of the
ROARING beasts.

One by one,
Eliot stops them
in their tracks.

He leads the
lions back
to the zoo…

…as the
crowds cheer.

Sometimes the Coast Guard call on his services.

"Help!" they shout. "A ship is about to CRASH onto the rocks!"

Luckily, Eliot is a champion swimmer.

THE RUBBER DUCKY

He dives into the towering waves,
grabs the anchor and tows the ship to safety,
as the sailors shout "Hurray!"

Sometimes the Queen
requires his assistance.
"A criminal mastermind
has **stolen** the royal jewels!"
announces the Royal Butler.

Luckily, Eliot is
an excellent sleuth.

He sneaks into the criminal mastermind's secret hideout.

Tip-toe!

He follows the clues, cracks the code, opens the safe...

...and return the jewels to the grateful Queen.

Tonight, Eliot receives an urgent message from the world's Most Important Scientists.

"A gigantic METEOR is heading this way! It's going to SMASH into the Earth!"

This is Eliot's most **important mission ever!**

Luckily, Eliot has built a Meteor-Busting Rocket Launcher for just such occasions.

Unluckily, it's hidden
    in a deep cave in the
mountains of **TIBET**.

The only way to get there
    before the meteor
strikes is by supersonic jet.
    Luckily, Eliot is a
skilled jet pilot.

Eliot sets off.
    Over the Alps.
Over the Caspian Sea.
    Across to the
Himalayas.

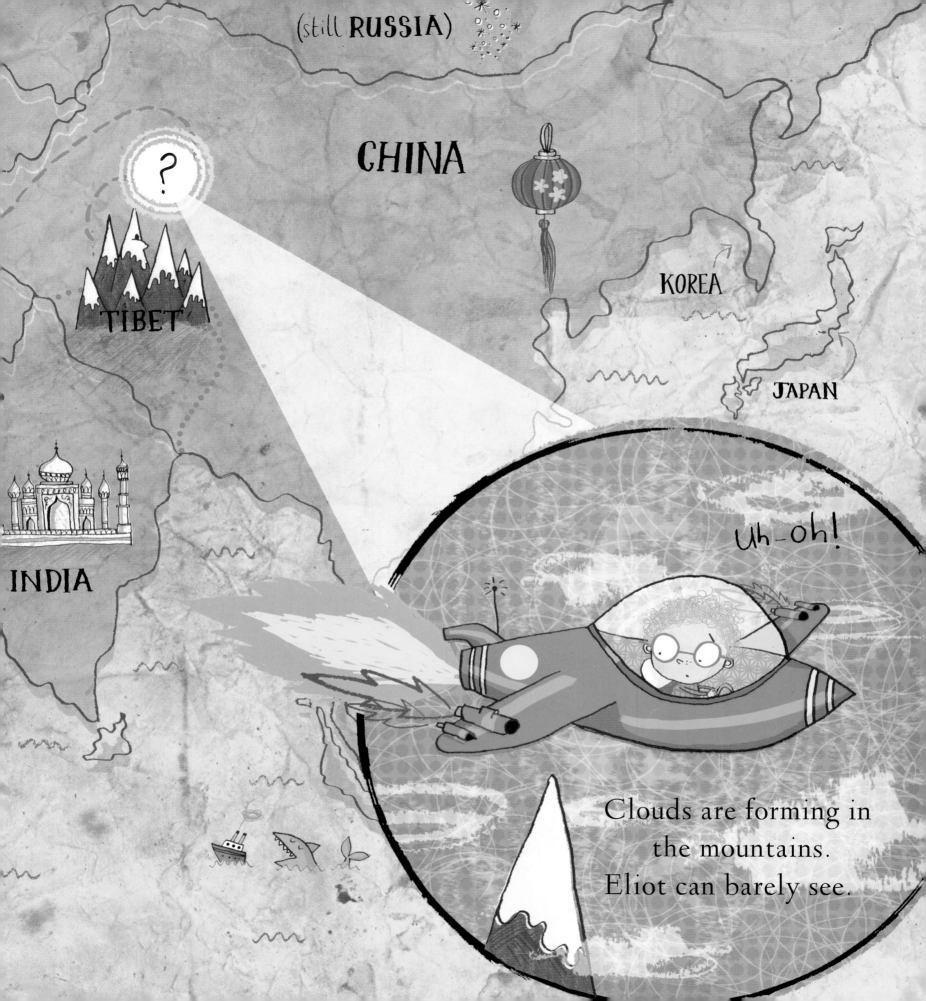

Suddenly a snow-capped peak
flashes past his window.
Another looms up straight ahead.
Eliot dips his left wing
and swerves just in time.

To reach the cave he must now
land on the shortest,
most dangerous
runway in the world.

He grips
 the controls.
The wheels
 bump the ground.

Screeech!
Eliot skids to a halt.

The sky is blazing with
the light of the meteor.

Closer
and
closer
it comes.

Eliot can see the entrance
to the cave, far above him.
Luckily, Eliot is a highly
experienced mountaineer.
He scrambles up the cliff face,
and into the cave.

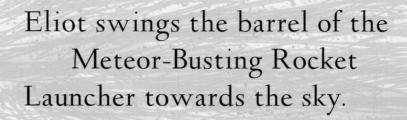

Eliot swings the barrel of the
Meteor-Busting Rocket
Launcher towards the sky.

He aims.
He holds his breath.
He waits until just
the right moment…

He fires!

KAPOW!

Eliot saves the world from destruction!

The Queen gives Eliot
an award for his
courage and ingenuity.

The Earth trembles
with deafening applause.

But being a
    Midnight Superhero
is very tiring.

It doesn't leave Eliot
    with much energy.
So by day...

Eliot is quiet.

shh!

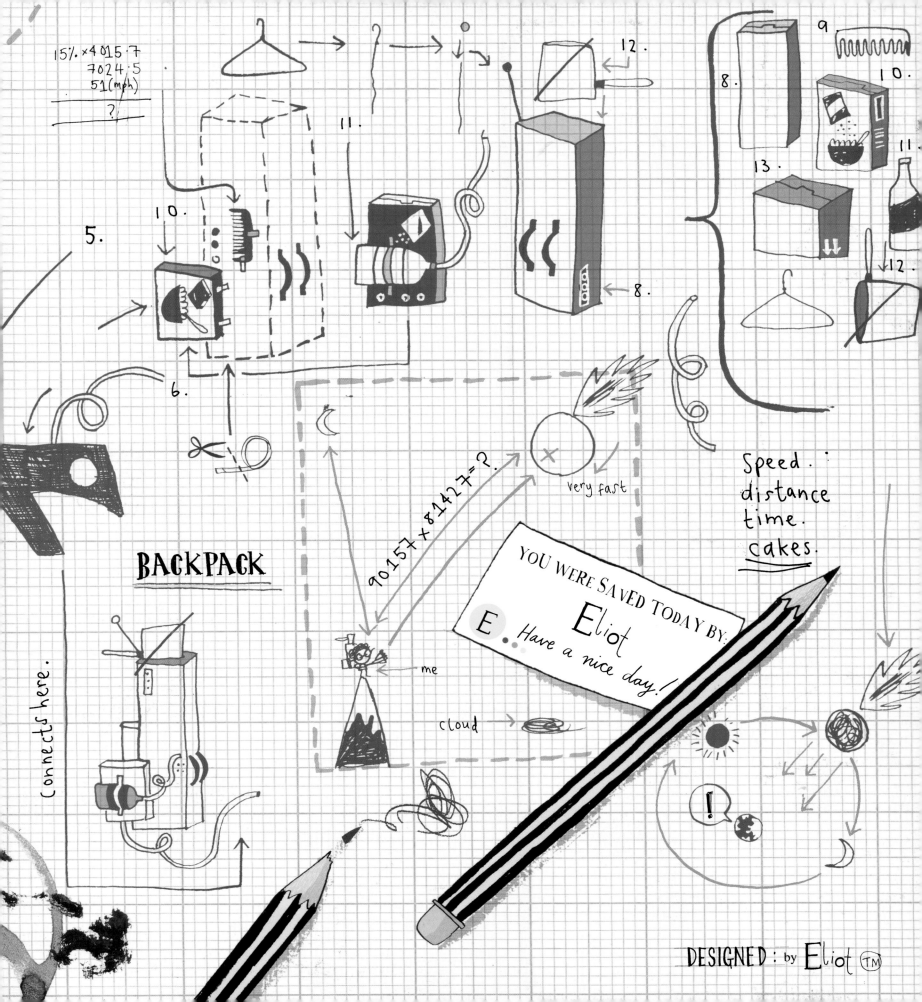